To

From

The Marvelous Maze

The Marvelous Maze

By Maxine Rose Schur

Illustrated by Patricia Dewitt-Grush & Robin Dewitt

Inquiries should be directed to
Stemmer House Publishers, Inc.
2627 Caves Road
Owings Mills, MD   21117

A Barbara Holdridge Book
Printed and bound in Hong Kong
First Edition

Library of Congress Cataloging in Publication Data

Schur, Maxine Rose
  The Marvelous Maze / by Maxine Rose Schur: illustrated by
Robin Dewitt and Patricia Dewitt-Grush. — 1st ed.
      p.   cm.
  "A Barbara Holdridge book"—T.p. verso.
  Summary: When a clever prince has a beautiful maze garden
constructed and decrees that he will marry the princess who can
find her way out, forty-three princesses try without success,
before the very different forty-fourth arrives.
  ISBN 0-88045-132-7 (alk. paper)
  [1. Princes—Fiction. 2. Princesses—Fiction. 3. Maze gardens-
-Fiction.] I. Dewitt, Robin, ill. II. Dewitt, Pat, ill.
III. Title.
PZ7.S3964Mar   1995   95-18333
                                                          CIP
                                                           AC

nce, long ago, there lived in a faraway kingdom an orphan prince named Edric. The prince was clever as a cat and brave as you please. Challenge him to leap across the drawbridge as it was closing—Prince Edric could do it. Dare him to shoot beans from the tower and hit the coachman on his bottom—Prince Edric could do it. Why, he could even solve a riddle standing on his head!

He could do everything, it seemed. Yet there were some things he could not even imagine. Without parents or playmates, he knew nothing of talking with others, sharing secrets or playing games. For never had he heard a true word of friendship or murmur of love, but only "Yes, Your Highness" and "As you wish, Young Sir."

Then one day, exactly a year before he was to be crowned king, the prince's chief advisor, Lord Elderbore, made an announcement.

"Every king needs a queen," he declared and handed the prince a fat scroll. "Here is a list of forty-four princesses. From this list you may choose a bride."

Prince Edric had been lonely for so long that he quite liked the idea of taking a bride. Yet he was afraid, too. *What if she were simple?* he thought to himself. A clever prince must have a clever princess! So Prince Edric immediately devised a test to make sure his wife would be clever. The princess who could pass the test would be his bride.

6

Prince Edric summoned the royal gardener.

"Burdock", he said, "plant me a garden of hedgerows that curl in and around like giant snakes. Make me a most marvelous maze, with one way in and another way out. The way out will be a secret—a secret only you and I will know."

Burdock did as he was commanded. When the garden was completed, he folded a paper into the prince's hand and said, "Here is the map of the maze, Your Highness. Guard it well."

Then Prince Edric ordered his heralds to proclaim this challenge throughout the land:

"The first princess who can find her way out of the maze will become my queen."

Soon, beautiful princesses from near and far arrived at the castle gates in their golden carriages. They came with special mirrors, compasses, sundials, maps and spyglasses. The princesses greeted the prince with low curtsies and high hopes of being the only one to find her way out of the maze.

The first to try, Princess Ephemera, twitched her fan nervously and combed her curls with the jade comb she snatched now and then from her droopy silk bag. The prince saw that she was nervous and shy, but not without beauty. He bade her enter the maze. Then, from his tower, he watched.

Princess Ephemera ran this way and that. She raced in circles, whirling around and about, all the while staring at her little compass as if it were an egg about to hatch. At last, with puppy-like cries, she collapsed in confusion on the ground. The prince sent Burdock to lead her out.

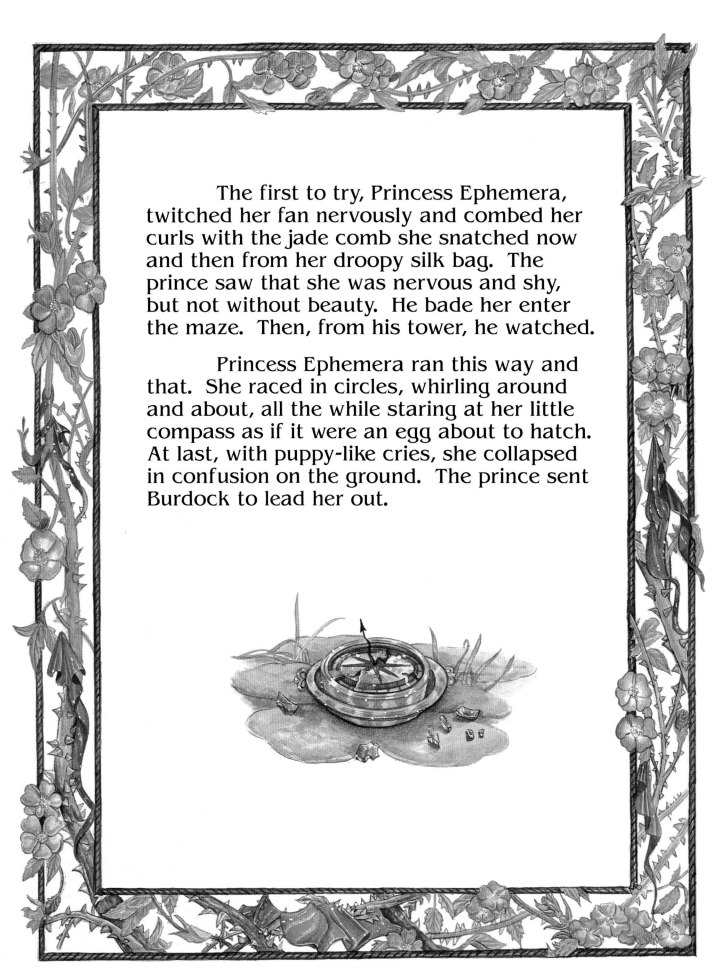

The twenty-third princess, Bisqueeta, had powdered her nose so much that it reminded the prince of a broken sugar cookie. She was both proud and clever. Like many of the princesses, she had devised a trick to find her way out. To avoid confusion, she unwound a spool of silver thread behind her, marking the paths she had already taken.

But the thread got caught in her fancy skirts. It tangled in the grass and twisted in the gorse bush. It bunched in hopeless knots about her feet. And so, like the others, this princess was led out in tatters and in tears.

Each day another princess was introduced to the prince. And each day another princess became lost in the merciless paths of the maze.

So the summer passed, until all but one name was crossed off Lord Elderbore's list. Prince Edric stared down at his maze and sighed. "Is there no clever princess in the kingdom?" he asked himself.

Weeks passed. Autumn came, then winter. Everyone had all but forgotten about the forty-fourth princess. It appeared that the prince's challenge had come to an end. He felt more alone than ever.

Then, one early summer day, a cloaked figure walked past the royal guards and knocked at the castle door. Her name was Gladwin. Round and plain as squash she was and carrying a miller's sack. Standing before the prince, she did not curtsy but extended her hand and said heartily, "I'm pleased to meet you."

Quickly, Prince Edric glanced down his list and there was the name "Princess Gladwin," the forty-fourth and last princess. *She is plain but not ugly,* the prince thought. *She is bold but not overbearing.* He bade her enter the maze, and at this she gave him a plump smile.

How slowly this princess walked! Here she stopped to sniff the morning-sweet smell of the briar roses. There she paused to watch a snail inch its way along the rough stone path. She walked around and about the maze, singing all the way. When at last she found herself in the center of the maze, she gathered in her simple skirt, spread out a blanket, took some bread and cheese from her sack and began to eat.

After her meal, the princess again reached into her sack and drew out neither a compass nor a map—but a book! She wrapped herself in the blanket and started to read. When the light faded, she shut her eyes and went to sleep.

But at noon she made another picnic and read another book. In the evening she appeared to be talking—or was it singing?—to the birds.

Night came again. The moon shone gently over the garden, lacing the paths with strips of silver. Untroubled, the princess spread out her blanket and went to sleep.

Prince Edric did not know what to make of her. Surely, he thought, she will give up by tomorrow. But tomorrow came and Princess Gladwin remained. There she sat, in the center of the maze—like a nut on a fruitcake.

The next morning, when Prince Edric looked from his tower, he saw she was braiding violets into her hair. It made a charming picture and the prince smiled in spite of himself.

She has a patience and a quiet charm that pleases me. I should like to know more about this forty-fourth princess.

Now he wished with all his heart the game would end. He wanted the princess to find her way out of the maze soon or send for help.

The prince grew impatient. He ordered Burdock to bring her to him. Within minutes the gardener returned.

"Her Highness says she will wait."

"Wait for what?"

"For you, Prince Edric," said Burdock. "She is waiting for Your Highness to escort her out."

Prince Edric stared at Burdock in disbelief. Suddenly, all his friendly feelings for the princess turned to dislike.

"What arrogance! What gall!" he said loudly. "I am the prince. I am almost a king. I do not take orders!"

"Yes, Your Highness," the gardener said and bowing low, he left.

The prince, miserable, stared down at the maze.

The sun rose and fell and rose again, but Princess Gladwin continued to wait. By the afternoon of the fourth day, the prince at last relented and agreed to escort the princess from the garden. It seemed the only way to get rid of her.

25

Prince Edric undid the latch and entered the maze. He strode angrily along the wide outer lanes. Right, left, left, right, left, right, right. The more he walked, the angrier he grew. And the faster he walked, the larger the maze became, as if it were unrolling itself like a scroll.

After endlessly looping in and out, he realized with horror that he was lost. And he'd forgotten the map! Prince Edric stumbled forward in confusion. *This is MY garden*, he reminded himself. *I cannot get lost in it.* But as the prince wandered around and around and around, this thought was of little comfort.

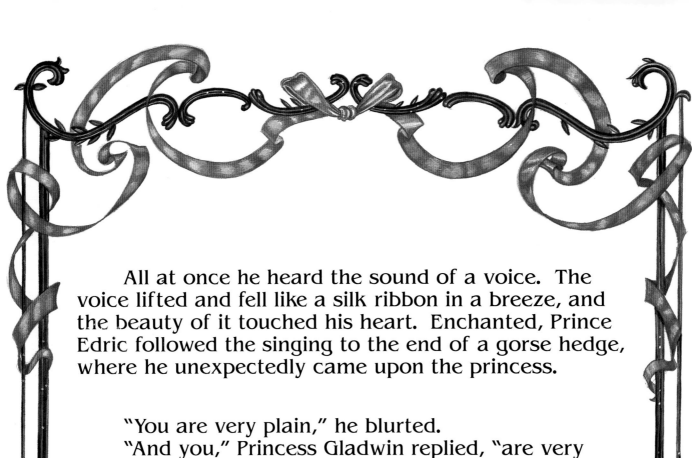

All at once he heard the sound of a voice. The voice lifted and fell like a silk ribbon in a breeze, and the beauty of it touched his heart. Enchanted, Prince Edric followed the singing to the end of a gorse hedge, where he unexpectedly came upon the princess.

"You are very plain," he blurted.
"And you," Princess Gladwin replied, "are very rude. However, I do thank you for my pleasant stay in your garden. Now I would like to leave."
"As you wish," the prince replied coolly.

In a princely manner, he offered her his hand, to lead. She accepted it.

They began to walk towards the palace. At first they went in silence, but soon the princess began to speak. She pointed out hedges decked with long white banners of honeysuckle. She showed him how to name the butterflies that danced around the gorse berries. And then, deep among the brambles, they both found a wren's nest made of moss and green willow.

Slowly, Prince Edric's anger turned to happiness. For the first time, the prince saw the beauty of his own garden.

"It's so green and so filled with life!" he exclaimed aloud. *Just like her eyes,* he added silently, surprising himself with this thought.

The sun began to slide down behind the hedges, but still the royal pair showed no sign of haste. Prince Edric, who once believed it wonderfully clever to get out of the garden, now wanted to stay there forever with Gladwin.

They walked, they talked, and the more they talked, the more slowly they walked—until in the end they stood like two close trees whispering to each other in the wind.

From the distant meadows came the day-end
sound of the shepherd's horn. Glancing up at the first
star of the evening, Prince Edric suddenly became
aware of time passing. "I don't know where we are,"
he confessed. "I know the directions of a few of these
paths but not all of them. Truly, we are lost!"

"Tush! I know the way out," Princess Gladwin said.
"You know the way out?" the prince asked in
amazement. "How can you?"

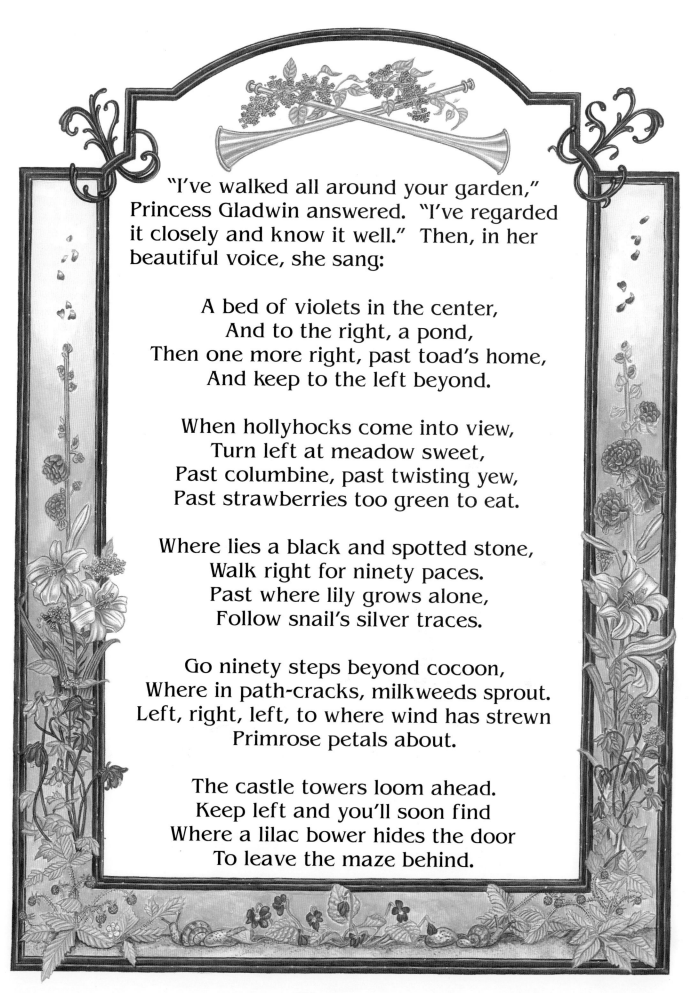

"I've walked all around your garden,"
Princess Gladwin answered. "I've regarded
it closely and know it well." Then, in her
beautiful voice, she sang:

A bed of violets in the center,
And to the right, a pond,
Then one more right, past toad's home,
And keep to the left beyond.

When hollyhocks come into view,
Turn left at meadow sweet,
Past columbine, past twisting yew,
Past strawberries too green to eat.

Where lies a black and spotted stone,
Walk right for ninety paces.
Past where lily grows alone,
Follow snail's silver traces.

Go ninety steps beyond cocoon,
Where in path-cracks, milkweeds sprout.
Left, right, left, to where wind has strewn
Primrose petals about.

The castle towers loom ahead.
Keep left and you'll soon find
Where a lilac bower hides the door
To leave the maze behind.

Princess Gladwin smiled up at his surprised face. Softly singing the song again, she took his hand to lead him out of his garden. The sky was now black, glittering with star candles. Over the garden a yellow moon hung low, like a paper lantern.

After a while, Prince Edric learned the song too, and he began to lead. So hand in hand, the prince and princess made their way slowly through the shadowy paths of the maze towards the lights of the palace. First she guiding him, then he guiding her.

On and on they went like this. Together. He guiding her, she guiding him.

Through the garden and ever after.

AUTHOR'S NOTE

In days of old, men and women of royal birth created elaborate mazes to delight and perplex their guests. By 1500, at the height of the Renaissance, more than 500 garden mazes flourished in the castle gardens of Europe.

It is told that in the early seventeenth century, a bored English prince planted a maze as a test of wits for his lady visitors. That maze has long since fallen into decay. But one who saw it wrote that "it is a most marvelous maze whose beauty is without rival anywhere on this earth."

For Lucia and Julia

Designed by Barbara Holdridge
Composed in Benguiat Book by David Chapman, Baltimore, Maryland
Title Calligraphy by Sally J. K. Davies
Printed on 80 lb. Matt Art acid-free paper and bound
by COLORCORP/Sing Cheong, Hong Kong

Tests
for use with

ALGEBRA 1

Third Edition

bju press®.com

270579

ISBN 978-1-60682-047-6

90000

9 781606 820476

Chapter 1

Sections 1 & 2

_____ 1. Which of the following are irrational numbers? List all correct answers.

 a. $\dfrac{\sqrt{3}}{2}$

 b. $\dfrac{\sqrt{9}}{2}$

 c. π

 d. -3.5

 e. $3.\overline{02}$

Let $R = \{2, 4, 6, 8, 10\}$ and $S = \{3, 6, 9, 12\}$.

_____ 2. Find $R \cap S$.

_____ 3. Find $R \cup S$.

Use the number line for questions 4 and 5.

_____ 4. Find the length of the segment from A to C.

_____ 5. State the coordinate of the opposite of B.

6. Describe the absolute value of a number.